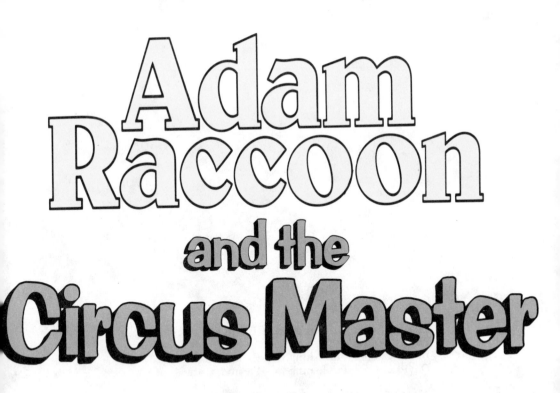

Adam Raccoon
and the
Circus Master

Glen Keane

Chariot Books
DAVID C. COOK PUBLISHING CO.

To Max

Chariot Books is an imprint of David C. Cook
Publishing Co.
David C. Cook Publishing Co., Elgin, Illinois 60120
David C. Cook Publishing Co., Weston, Ontario

ADAM RACCOON AND THE CIRCUS MASTER
© 1987 by Glen Keane for text and illustrations

First printing, 1987
Printed in U.S.A.
95 94 93   15 14 13 12 11 10

Library of Congress Cataloging-in-Publication Data

Keane, Glen, 1954-
    Adam Raccoon and the circus master.

    (Parables for kids)
    Summary: Adam Raccoon leaves his comfortable home
in the Master's Wood and runs away to join the circus,
where he eventually finds himself regretting his decision.
    [1. Raccoons—Fiction. 2. Circus—Fiction. 3. Parables]
I. Title. II. Series.
PZ7.K2173Ag   1987   [E]   86-26889
ISBN 1-55513-090-9

Master's Wood was filled with the wonderful aromas of dinnertime. At King Aren's home, he and Adam Raccoon had just sat down to eat.

Living with King Aren, Adam
Raccoon enjoyed many good things.

He especially loved lying by the fire,
listening as King Aren would tell him stories.

During the day, Adam would work
with the king and save the money he
earned in his piggy bank.

They were like father and son.
Nothing could make Adam leave King
Aren, or so he thought.

That night a circus train echoed
across Master's Wood.
"Whooo! Whooo!"

With a hiss of steam and smoke, the train came to a stop.

By morning what once was only a
field now held a circus.

Adam was
thrilled to find
a circus poster.

All day he imagined himself as a great circus performer.

When night came, Adam was too
excited to sleep. *How wonderful the
circus must be!* he thought.

Carefully, so as not to wake King
Aren, he took his piggy bank . . .

and ran away to the bright lights
of the circus.

As Adam entered the circus, he was amazed. He had never seen anything like this before in Master's Wood.

He watched with wonder as he saw
the strong man perform.

And cheered as the Ferris wheel
whirled him around.

But his favorite was the big top!

Adam decided to ask the circus master if he could join the circus.

"What can you do?" the circus master asked gruffly.

"Watch!" Adam said and started
to juggle.

"Sure, you can join. But it'll cost
you plenty!" the circus master said as
he grabbed the piggy bank.

But Adam didn't mind. He became a
great juggler and the crowds loved him.

Adam was a success! Soon he had
forgotten all about King Aren.

But King Aren had not forgotten about Adam. Each day he would watch, waiting for Adam to return home.

Then one night, when Adam went to perform, he found he had been replaced.

The circus master led Adam to a
large tent in the back of the circus.
"Here's your new job," he said. "Go
on in. Your audience is waiting."

"I don't understand!" Adam said. "You want me to entertain all these muddy circus elephants?"

"I don't want you to entertain them. I want you to *clean* them!" the circus master laughed.

Working late into the night, Adam
scrubbed the elephants, one by one.

He was made to sleep on the floor of
the monkeys' cage.

At mealtime, Adam's only food was
the monkeys' throwaway
banana peels.

At night his tummy growled with hunger as he remembered how he always had enough to eat with King Aren.

Adam realized he had been wrong to leave King Aren, and decided to go back to him.

But Adam could not open the cage door. It was locked.

The monkeys decided to help. "Hey, Jumbo, can you get the circus master's key for us?" the head monkey asked.

"Sure!
No problem!"
the big elephant said.

The circus master was barking out orders and did not notice the elephant's trunk reaching into his pocket for the key.

The elephant handed the key to the
monkey, who opened the lock.

Adam was free! Hopping off the train, he thanked the animals and headed for home.

As Adam got closer to home, he started to worry. "Will King Aren take me back?" he wondered.

But while Adam was still a long way off . . .

King Aren saw him and ran to meet
him with outstretched arms.

As King Aren
hugged him,
Adam knew
he was forgiven.

King Aren invited everyone to a party to celebrate Adam's return. It was hard to tell who was happier— Adam, who was with King Aren again, or King Aren, whose son had come home.

Do you find yourself telling your children stories to help them understand things you want them to learn or remember? Maybe you find yourself remembering the point of a sermon because of the illustration used.

Telling stories to convey truth is not new. Jesus often taught in parables.

Why do we use parables to teach? Because we *remember* stories—and the truths they hold.

Adam Raccoon and King Aren illustrate truths from God's Word in language and experiences children readily understand. While stories like these are not a substitute for the Bible, they will enhance and reinforce the Bible teaching your children receive.

What does it mean to repent and ask forgiveness for sins? *Adam Raccoon and the Circus Master* illustrates this as Adam runs away to join the circus and then returns home to King Aren.

Children may recognize the parallels between Adam and the Prodigal Son. Both take their money and follow what seems to be an exciting life. Soon, both have spent their fortunes. Adam realizes that washing dirty elephants and eating the monkeys' garbage is a far cry from the rich life he had with King Aren.

But will the King take him back? Of course he will. Children need to understand that when they stray, God is always willing and ready to take them back. He's a forgiving God when they return and say, as the Prodigal did, "Father, I have sinned."

After reading about Adam Raccoon, read the story of the Prodigal in Luke 15:11-32.

Discuss the stories with your children. Ask, "What might tempt you to run away from God?" Children need to understand that there are other ways to stray than actually to run away from home.

Talk about ways that they might "run away," such as spending time with friends who are bad influences on them. Help children to think of situations they face that tempt them to sin.

Be ready to pray with your children if they are convicted of sin, and let them know that you, too, forgive them.